W9-CBJ-232

Sleep Tight

By Constance Allen
Illustrated by David Prebenna

"Sesame Workshop"®, "Sesame Street"®, and associated characters, trademarks, and design elements are owned and licensed by Sesame Workshop. ©2014, 1991 Sesame Workshop. All Rights Reserved.

Published by Bendon, Ashland, OH 44805
bendonpub.com
1-888-5-BENDON

No part of this book may be reproduced or copied in any form without written permission from the copyright owner.

Printed in China
82008-TG F 0514

"Time to go home, Elmo!" calls Elmo's daddy.

"Just one more game of monster tag, please, Daddy?" asks Elmo.

"Okay. One more game," says Elmo's daddy.

On the way home from the park, Elmo
and his daddy see lots of other people
on their way home, too.
It's almost bedtime for little monsters.

EAT AT
JOE'S

On Sesame Street, everyone is getting ready for bed.

Splish, splash! Little Bird shakes his feathers in his warm bath.

Sleepy monsters comb their fur
and brush their teeth.

Oscar finishes his book, *Mother Grouch Rhymes*.
  "Little Boy Grouch, come blow your kazoo.
  Take a mud bath and eat anchovy stew..."
He closes his book.
Sleep tight, sleepy grouch.

Big Bird sings his teddy bear a lullaby.
"Rock-a-bye, Radar, snug in my nest.
Time for us both to lie down and rest!
Sleep tight, little bear," says Big Bird.

In the Count's castle, the Count counts sheep.
"One sheep! Two sheep! Three beautiful
woolly sheep!" cries the Count.
Sleep tight, Count.

In the country, Cowboy Grover settles down to sleep under the stars.

"Sleep tight, little cows!" he calls.

In the city, Hoots the Owl plays a saxophone serenade above the city lights.

Bee-boop-a-diddly-diddly-doo-wha-doo!

"I'll keep things cool till morning," he croons. "Sleep tight, everyone."

In Ernie's window box, sleepy
Twiddlebugs snuggle under their leaf blankets.
Sleep tight, little Twiddlebugs.

All is quiet on Sesame Street. Monsters and
birds and grouches and Twiddlebugs sleep
soundly in their beds.

Sleep tight, little Elmo.